W9-CKH-422

NORMAL PUBLIC LIBRARY

A12004 154402

For P. B.

And to the (very silly) bear on the hill in Yosemite Park—you know who you are!

Text and illustrations copyright © Jan Fearnley 2001

All rights reserved. No part of this publication may be reproduced or transmitted in any form or by any means, electronic or mechanical, including photocopy, recording, or any information storage and retrieval system, without permission in writing from the publisher.

Requests for permission to make copies of any part of the work should be mailed to the following address:
Permissions Department, Harcourt, Inc., 6277 Sea Harbor Drive, Orlando, Florida 32887-6777.

First published in Great Britain in 2001 by Egmont Books Limited, 239 Kensington High Street, London W8 6SA
First U.S. edition 2002

www.HarcourtBooks.com

Library of Congress Cataloging-in-Publication Data
Fearnley, Jan.
A perfect day for it/Jan Fearnley.
p. cm.
Summary: Bear announces that it's "a perfect day for it" and his friends follow him up the mountain, each imagining what special treat they might share there, but all come to agree that Bear's "it" is just right.
[1. Bears—Fiction. 2. Animals—Fiction. 3. Snow—Fiction. 4. Sledding—Fiction. 5. Friendship—Fiction.] I. Title.
PZ7.F2965Pe 2002   [E]—dc21   2001006871   ISBN 0-15-216634-3

A C E G H F D B

Printed in Singapore

DISCARD

A Perfect Day for It

Jan Fearnley

NORMAL PUBLIC LIBRARY
NORMAL, ILLINOIS

Harcourt, Inc.

SAN DIEGO   NEW YORK   LONDON

It was a beautiful, crisp winter morning. Bear stepped outside and sniffed all around him. His merry little eyes twinkled in the bright light. His big furry feet crunched the fresh white snow under his toes. He licked a claw and held it into the chill morning breeze.

"Perfect!" he said.
Bear had a plan.

"Good morning, Bear," said Badger. "Where are you going?"

"Up the mountain," Bear replied.

"What for?" Badger asked nosily.

"Because it's a perfect day for it," said Bear, and off he went tramp tramp **tramp** up the snowy mountain track.

"He's up to something," said Badger. "I bet he's going to look for his secret stash of honeycomb!"

Badger's mouth watered at the thought of sweet, sticky honey oozing from the comb.

"Such a shame to let Bear search on his own. I'd better go along to help."

So Badger went scritchity scratchity up the hill, hurrying to catch Bear,

and Bear went
tramp tramp tramp
up the snowy mountain track.

Fox was outside his den shoveling snow when his keen yellow eyes spotted Bear and Badger.

"They're up to something!" he said. "I bet they're planning to snowball someone! What fun! But they'll need a sharp eye and some cunning. I'd better go along, too."

So Fox went paddypaw paddypaw,

Badger went scritchity scratchity,

and Bear went
tramp tramp tramp
up the snowy mountain track.

Squirrel was sitting in the treetops when she saw her friends climbing higher and higher up the mountain.

"They're up to something!" she said. "I bet they're looking for treasure!"

Squirrel thought about her own treasure store of nuts buried at the foot of her tree. She felt very excited.

"I'm an expert at finding treasure, and they'll be hopeless. I'd better go along to help."

So squirrel scampered down her tree tippytoes **tippytoes** and followed her friends,

ₚₐddypaw paddypaw,

and tramp tramp tramp up the snowy mountain track.

scritchity scratchity,

Squirrel was in such a hurry, she nearly
trod on Mole as she ran past.

"They're up to something!" said Mole.
"I bet they're off to find some worms!"

Mole's tummy rumbled at the thought of some tasty worms.

"Yum yum, my favorite!" he said.
"I'd better go, too." And he slid along the
icy path after his friends—slippy slidey bump!

NORMAL PUBLIC LIBRARY
NORMAL, ILLINOIS

Slippy slidey bump!

Tippytoes tippytoes,

paddypaw paddypaw,

scritchity scratchity,

and tramp tramp tramp
up the snowy mountain track.

Bear got quite a surprise when he
finally looked back over his shoulder
and discovered he was being followed.
He chuckled and kept on climbing.

Up, up, up he went, until he had
reached the summit. Then he stopped.

"Perfect!" he said to himself, and sat down on his big furry bottom for a little rest. He looked at the beautiful view—the trees, the valley...

…and the excited faces of his friends as they crowded all around him.

"Where's the honeycomb?" asked Badger.

"Honeycomb? What about the snowballing?" asked Fox.

"What about the worms?" asked Mole.

"Worms! What kind of treasure is that?" asked Squirrel. "Yuck!"

"I never said I was climbing up here for any of those things," said Bear.

"But you said it was a perfect day for it," Badger grumbled. "So we've come all this way for nothing! It's very cold up here, you know."

Bear threw back his big shaggy head and laughed so loudly it echoed around the valley.

"What's so funny?" asked the others.

"But it *is* a perfect day for it," chuckled Bear. "Climb aboard, and I'll show you."

Bear lay on his tummy, and his friends clambered onto his broad furry back.

"Now," said Bear, "it really is a perfect, wonderful, truly magnificent day, and the best reason I know for climbing up the mountain is…

...so you can slide back down again!

Hold on tight!"

NORMAL PUBLIC LIBRARY
NORMAL, ILLINOIS